Museum
Kittens

The Pharaoh's Curse

HOLLY

Illustrated

LITTLE TIGER

LONDON

Ground Floor

Museum

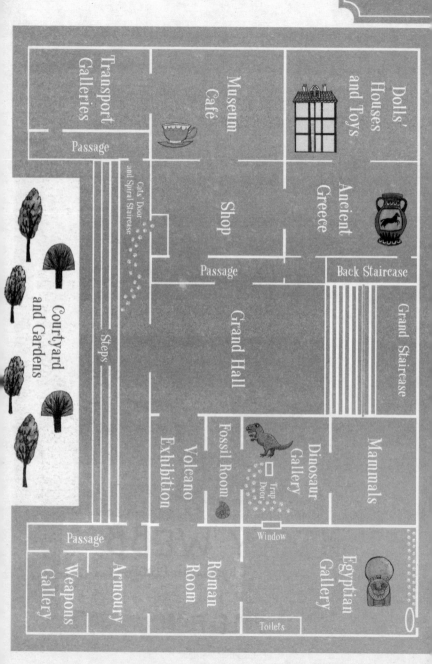

Transport Galleries

Museum Café

Dolls' Houses and Toys

Passage

Shop

Ancient Greece

Cats' Door and Spiral Staircase

Passage

Back Staircase

Courtyard and Gardens

Grand Hall

Grand Staircase

Steps

Mammals

Fossil Room

Dinosaur Gallery

Trap Door

Volcano Exhibition

Window

Passage

Weapons Gallery

Armoury

Roman Room

Egyptian Gallery

Toilets

Museum
Kittens

For my readers in St Petersburg – HW

For Alby and Neri – SL

STRIPES PUBLISHING LIMITED
An imprint of the Little Tiger Group
1 Coda Studios, 189 Munster Road,
London SW6 6AW

A paperback original
First published in Great Britain in 2020

Text copyright © Holly Webb, 2020
Illustrations copyright © Sarah Lodge, 2020
Author photograph copyright © Charlotte Knee Photography

ISBN: 978-1-78895-188-3

The Forest Stewardship Council® (FSC®) is a global, not-for-profit organization
dedicated to the promotion of responsible forest management worldwide. FSC®
defines standards based on agreed principles for responsible forest stewardship
that are supported by environmental, social, and economic stakeholders.
To learn more, visit www.fsc.org

10 9 8 7 6 5 4 3 2 1

Map

First Floor

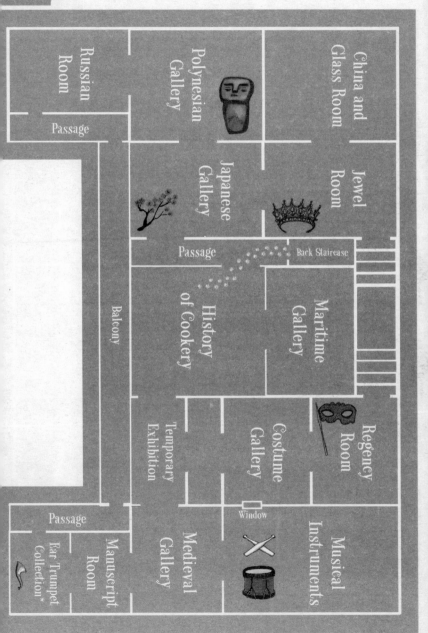

Russian Room

Passage

Polynesian Gallery

China and Glass Room

Jewel Room

Japanese Gallery

Passage

Back Staircase

Balcony

History of Cookery

Maritime Gallery

Temporary Exhibition

Costume Gallery

Regency Room

Window

Passage

Manuscript Room

Ear Trumpet Collection

Medieval Gallery

Musical Instruments

Mrs Jane Martlesham Bequest

❧ Chapter One ❧

"What are they all so excited about?"
Boris whispered to Peter and his sisters.
He was peering round the huge, painted
mummy case that hid the tunnel down to
the cellars, where the museum cats lived.

The Egyptian Gallery was full of
museum staff, talking in whispers as
they opened up a large packing case and
started to unwrap something that had

been inside. The elderly professor who ran the Egyptology department was actually squeaking with delight.

"Is it jewels?" Bianca asked hopefully, pushing the large ginger kitten out of the way so she could see.

"It could be one of those golden masks that the pharaohs had in their tombs," the small tabby Tasha suggested, slinking further round the mummy case to look. "It must be something very special."

"Gold…" Bianca purred. "Diamonds too? Maybe pearls?"

"I don't think so," said Tasha. "The masks are mostly gold and lapis lazuli – that lovely blue stone. The ancient Egyptians used it a lot."

2

"Hmf! Blue stone." Bianca looked disappointed and her white tail drooped. "Not as nice as diamonds. But I do like gold."

"*That* doesn't look like a jewelled golden *anything*," Peter pointed out. The black kitten had given up trying to see round Boris and crawled underneath him instead. "It's just … a bit of paper."

"Huh? That's not a treasure!" Bianca said crossly.

"What are you lot looking at?"

All four kittens skittered sideways in surprise as Grandpa Ivan appeared behind them. He was the oldest of the cats, white and long-haired with a great drooping moustache of whiskers, his ears looked chewed and he only had one eye. But he knew everything that was going on in the museum and he was very good at sneaking up on the kittens. "Ah, it's arrived then!"

"Do you know what it is?" Boris asked. "It doesn't look very exciting but the museum people are making a lot of fuss about it. They're putting it in an enormous glass case, look!"

"It's a temporary loan from a museum on the other side of the country," Grandpa

Ivan explained. "They're rebuilding their Egyptian Galleries so they're lending out their precious exhibits. It's part of the *Book of the Dead*."

"The what?" Tasha squeaked.

"The *Book of the Dead*." Grandpa Ivan chuckled. "It's a set of ancient magic spells for how to get safely to the afterlife, written out on great long strips of papyrus. That's paper made of reeds, you know."

Tasha nodded intelligently and the other kittens tried to look as though they knew what he meant too. All four of them were gazing at the strange piece of paper in fascination. Ancient magic spells!

"The Egyptians used to put copies of it into people's tombs so the spirits would know what to do. The scrolls were expensive, though, so they were mostly made for royalty and important officials. This one came from the tomb of a pharaoh, Thutmose I, so it's very grand, with beautiful pictures. This isn't the whole thing, of course. Only a little bit of the scroll is left. All the tombs were raided by thieves many times – and you can imagine that a long roll of papyrus is quite delicate."

"Hang on... This is a list of instructions for *ghosts*?" Boris looked shocked.

"Mmmm, not quite. I think they'd only be ghosts if they got it wrong," Grandpa Ivan said thoughtfully. "Mind you, no one's quite sure where Thutmose I's body ended up... He had at least three different coffins. But what's really special about this bit of papyrus is that no one knows what it means. Most of the *Book of the Dead* has been translated – it's all written in hieroglyphics, you know. Picture writing. But this part of the book is tricky to read, apparently, and this is the only copy that's ever been found! I heard the staff talking about it in the café. They're pretty sure it's a spell to do with a magical amulet – or it could be a curse on anyone who steals it..."

"I don't like the sound of that," Peter muttered, his whiskers shivering. "What if it's bad luck for it to be here in the museum?"

"There's no such thing as bad luck!" Tasha gave him a grown-up sort of look. No one was exactly sure how old Peter was. He had been left at the museum as an orphan, so the other kittens liked to think he was the littlest. "Spells and curses are all nonsense. And even if they weren't, this one is thousands of years old! Its power must have run out by now."

"Or it's spent years and years getting worse and worse," Boris growled, and Peter nodded at him, round-eyed.

Tasha sighed. Really, the other kittens were all so superstitious. She knew there was absolutely nothing to be worried about.

On the other side of the gallery, someone else was eyeing up the new exhibit too. Four rats were peeking out of a hole in the skirting board. It was a very small hole and they had to keep elbowing each other out of the way.

"What do you think it is?"

"Dunno, but it's got to be something good. Look at that case! Look how thick the glass is!"

"Definitely special. See all the fuss they're making. And did you spot those horrible cats over there? Behind the mummy? They've got their eyes on it too."

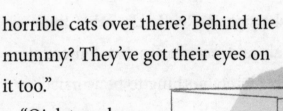

"Oi, let me have a look! Do you think it's something specially *delicious*?"

"Got to be. And look, you can see it's all nibbled around the edges. Someone's already had a taste."

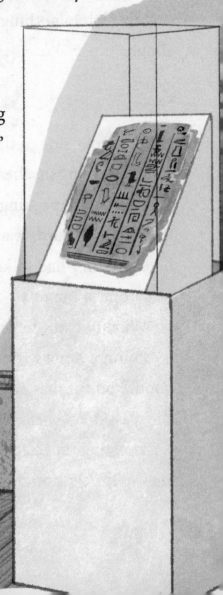

The rat leader nodded. "Well, there we are," he said, looking round at them all. "We can't let those mangy cats have it then, can we? We'd better start making a plan…"

News of the special new exhibit in the Egyptian Gallery began to spread around the museum. And so did rumours about the curse.

The lorry that had brought the old artefacts to the museum had got two flat tyres and suffered a mysterious engine failure on the way, the café staff muttered.

Then the day after the papyrus arrived, one of the guards slipped over in the gallery and banged his head on the display case. He said he didn't know how he'd done it – he was fine one minute and on the floor the next. All the water pipes started to make strange whistling noises and there were eerie shrieking sounds whenever anyone flushed the loo in the washrooms by the Egyptian Gallery.

The day after that, a school trip came to visit and one of the children was sick all over the floor. The cleaners said there was *definitely* a curse.

"I told you," Peter whispered to Tasha as they sat watching the others practise hunting one evening after the museum had closed. "That papyrus is bad news. The pharaoh doesn't like it being here! Grandpa Ivan said no one knows where

Thutmose I's mummy ended up and I bet his ghost's furious! Something really awful's going to happen to the museum!"

"No, it isn't," Tasha said, rolling her eyes. "Is it my turn yet?" she added, twitching her tail. But Boris was already creeping forwards in a hunting crouch.

"Very good," Grandpa Ivan growled. "And wait … wait and watch… Don't spring… I said *don't* spring, you ginger oaf!"

Boris tumbled head over heels and landed with a meaty thump. Then he glared at the others. Bianca was smirking, and he could tell Tasha and Peter were trying not to laugh. Peter's black muzzle was all wrinkled up with the strain of holding it in.

"Are you all right, dear?" their mother
Smoke murmured, nudging him gently.

"Yes," Boris muttered as he stood up.
Why did being the biggest and strongest
of the kittens always mean that he was

the clumsiest too. They were all supposed to be practising their ratting skills so they could grow up to be museum guard cats, like their mother and their grandfather and all their aunts and uncles. Boris knew that one of these days he was going to be a mighty hunter. He just needed to grow into his paws first.

"Have a rest, Boris," Smoke said. "Tasha, you try. Imagine a great grey rat, sneaking along the edge of the wall. You spot him…"

Tasha tensed up, her ears pricking and her tail beginning to swish from side to side. Boris watched her slinking towards the imaginary rat and sighed. She looked so … *professional*. At the moment, it seemed that the only way *he'd* ever catch a rat would be if he fell on top of it.

Perhaps it was because he'd eaten so much supper, Boris thought sadly to himself. He *was* quite full – maybe that's why he was so clumsy. He wished they didn't have to have lessons in the evenings but Smoke and Grandpa Ivan wanted them to practise hunting in the galleries where they would be real guard cats one day. So that meant they had to wait until the visitors had left.

Tasha prowled across the room, trying to imagine a rat, all sharp teeth and beady black eyes. Hunting imaginary rats was one thing but the thought of facing off against a fully grown rat was terrifying. Boris said he'd seen rats that were twice her size.

"Keep low!" her
mother called, and
Tasha crouched down even further,
paws trembling with the effort.

"Nicely done, nicely done," Grandpa
Ivan purred. "Very good form there,
small grey stripey one."

"She's Tasha." Smoke let out a sigh.

"I know perfectly well who she is. Now,
back, back, as fast as you can!"

Tasha whirled round and shot across
the gallery, claws scritching on the
slippery floor. She just managed to skid
to a stop before she crashed into the
other kittens.

"Hmmm. Yes. Well done." Grandpa
nodded regally and Tasha glowed. She
wasn't used to being told she was good

at things – she usually got told off for daydreaming during their hunting lessons. It was hard not to daydream when they were surrounded by so many beautiful things.

Peter prowled across the gallery to take his turn, and Tasha sat down and started to lick her paws and swipe them across her ears. Then she looked sideways at the tall plinth towering over them all.

The bronze statue of Bastet, the cat goddess, was one of her favourite museum treasures. It was more than two and a half thousand years old but the cat goddess looked just like so many cats that Tasha knew. On her best, tidiest days, Tasha hoped that she looked a little like the statue too.

She had read the sign on the plinth and she knew that Bastet was the Egyptian goddess of a great many things – secrets and songs and protection and happiness. But mostly cats.

"Thank you," Tasha whispered to the statue. "Did you help? I'm not usually very good at lessons."

The bronze cat stared silently ahead and her gold earrings glittered in the dim light. Tasha wished that she wasn't in a glass case. The cat was old and precious and delicate, Tasha knew that, but it would be so wonderful to nuzzle up against her, just once. Tasha couldn't help feeling that Bastet's hard bronze skin would melt to soft tabby-brown fur and she'd nudge back.

"You see, look at that, Boris," Tasha heard Grandpa Ivan say sternly. "Perfect hunting from little-black-kitten-I-can-never-remember-the-name-of. Practice! Practice, that's all it takes! Learn to control your paws!"

"Yes, Grandpa," Boris muttered, and Tasha gently brushed whiskers with him.

She didn't think Boris had been that bad.

"I'm always falling over my paws," she whispered to him.

"I've never been so hopeless before." Boris heaved a sigh. "I reckon it's that horrible bit of paper." He glared at the papyrus in its glass case. "It's cursed all right."

"No, it isn't!" Tasha hissed, but then her whiskers twitched worriedly.

Something was wrong, she could feel it. Peter was marching proudly towards them across the gallery – but then his ears began to flatten back and the fur stiffened up all along his spine.

There was a strange creaking noise and somehow Peter's shining black fur seemed to turn grey all at once. Tasha looked up slowly towards the ceiling and saw a great dark crack spread across the white plaster, branching out like the rivers on the maps she'd studied in the Map Room. Dust shimmered down like a waterfall.

"Run!" Boris yowled, and Peter scrambled out of the way just as the middle of the ceiling collapsed. Huge chunks of plaster crashed to the floor, right where he'd been standing.

"Peter!" Tasha mewed, nuzzling anxiously at him. And then she looked back at the gallery and whispered, "The treasures! Bastet's statue! The mummy cases! The papyrus!"

"All of you, out of here," Smoke hissed, herding the kittens to the safety of the doorway. They scurried along in front of her, glancing back at the scene of devastation, but it was hard to see anything through the haze of dust.

"Are you all right?" Boris asked Peter worriedly as Bianca tried to groom the dust out of his black fur. He was a small, skinny grey kitten instead of a small, skinny black kitten now.

"There's no point licking him," Grandpa Ivan told her. "What he needs is a bath."

Peter stared at Grandpa in horror but the old white cat was already thinking about more important things. "Where's that caretaker when we want him?" he muttered. "Lazy so-and-so. He should have come running... Ah..."

Grandpa Ivan's whiskers bristled and the kittens looked round to see the Old Man hurrying through the Roman Room. He was carrying a radio, gabbling into it as he ran. He stopped in the doorway, staring at the pile of plaster with eyes as round as marbles.

"About time," Smoke muttered. "On your way, kittens. We don't want the Old Man thinking we've got anything to do with this."

"He already does," Peter whispered back.

"Look. He's glaring at us."

The three other kittens peered round and saw that Peter was right. The elderly caretaker was eyeing the cats suspiciously.

"How can he think we've broken the ceiling?" Boris asked indignantly. Then he scowled at Tasha and the others, who were looking at each other meaningfully. "That's not fair! I've *never* broken a ceiling. It was only a smallish sort of dinosaur. And we put it all back together before anyone noticed!"

❧ Chapter Two ❧

The Old Man seemed to stare suspiciously at the kittens every time he saw them after that. And Boris was absolutely sure they weren't given as much food as usual either.

"There was hardly any breakfast!" he complained to Peter as they sneaked upstairs the next morning to spy on all the interesting goings-on in the Egyptian Gallery. Tasha and Bianca had already hurried off to see what was happening. "No nice meaty bits. Just that horrible brown biscuit stuff. He's paying us back because he thinks we did something to the ceiling. I told Tasha that papyrus was cursed! We have to do something now it's spoiling our breakfast – the most important meal of the day! Things are getting really serious."

"It tasted all right to me," Peter said.

Boris shook his head sadly. Peter had arrived at the museum in the middle of a rainstorm a few weeks before. Until then, the black kitten had been living on the streets and he'd always been hungry. Boris couldn't imagine what that would be like. But really, even a street cat ought to be able to tell the difference between manky cat biscuits and a lovely bit of fish.

Last night, whoever the Old Man had been talking to on his radio had turned up in a hurry and brought a whole lot of fussy people with clipboards. Grandpa Ivan had come back down to the cellars looking worried.

"They're going to close the Egyptian Gallery and the Roman Room until the ceiling's been mended," he'd explained to the other cats. The four kittens had curled up in their nest of old tapestries, pretending to be asleep but listening with all their ears.

There had been an anxious chorus of mews – the Egyptian Gallery was very popular with visitors. Shutting it down was going to make a lot of people really cross.

Now Boris and Peter crept under the portable screens the museum staff had put up at the door between the Roman Room and the rest of the museum. There were all sorts of strange noises coming from the Egyptian Gallery – bangs and screeches and occasional shouting. It didn't sound like their museum at all. Usually an unruly school party was the noisiest it got.

"Ooooh, out of the way," Peter squeaked as the screen was pulled back and two burly men staggered by. The two kittens squished themselves against the wall to avoid their stomping boots. The museum staff couldn't see above the huge box they were carrying.

"Where are they going with that?" Boris wondered.

"I suppose they want to get the precious things out of the way," Peter said, peering thoughtfully across the Roman Room. "Do you think they're moving everything? Some of those mummy cases are huge. And what about that stone sarcophagus? They'd need a crane!"

"A crane…" Boris purred excitedly. "Do you think so? I've never seen a crane." Then he nudged Peter. "If they've got builders in to mend the ceiling, there could be all sorts of things! Drills! Cement mixers! Maybe an angle grinder!"

Peter stared at him. "I don't even know what that is."

Boris lowered his head. "It's for cutting things… I like machines," he admitted.

"Mmmm." Peter eyed the bustling scene in the Egyptian Gallery. "Well. We'd better be careful. I don't think they're going to want us in there. And your mother did tell us to stay out of their way. She said everyone would be busy and we shouldn't bother them."

"I don't see why we can't be here," Boris said, but he didn't meet Peter's eyes. "We're only making sure no rats get in, aren't we? I wouldn't put anything past those nasty creatures. They're probably planning an attack on the mummies right this minute!"

He marched forwards, tail high, and Peter sighed and scurried after him.

The Egyptian Gallery was full of people. The elderly professor was standing in the middle, directing her staff, who were frantically packing huge crates or putting wooden frames around the exhibits that were too big to move easily. They seemed to be clearing out the middle of the gallery under the fallen bit of ceiling. The kittens had seen most of the people from the museum before, from a distance, but there were strangers here too. A big platform built of metal bars had appeared in the middle of the gallery and there were three builders in hard hats standing on it, staring at the ceiling.

"A scaff tower!" Boris gave a little purr

of bliss. "I've always wanted to go up a scaff tower."

"How do you *know* all this stuff?" Peter asked.

Boris shrugged. "Well… I like things that move and make noises and go fast… Big things…" He looked longingly at the scaffolding tower again. "Do you think they'd let us go up there?"

"No." Peter shook his whiskers firmly.

"I suppose you're right." Boris sighed. "Oh well." Then his ears twitched and he started forwards. "Hey, look! It's Bianca. She's up there already!"

Peter's ears flickered worriedly. The white kitten was up on top of the tower, winding herself round the ankles of a tall man in a suit

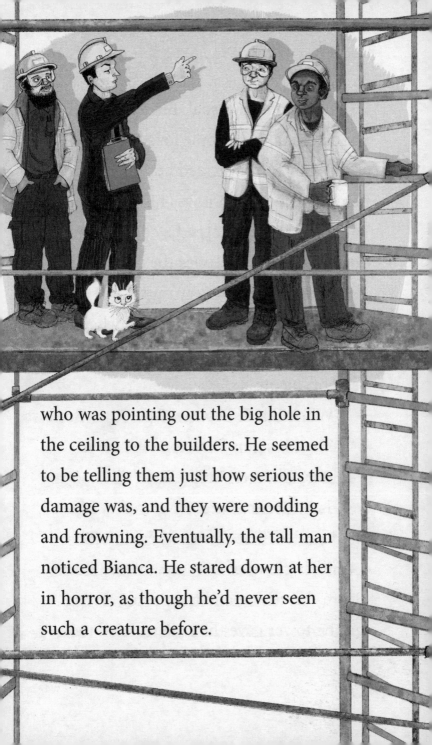

who was pointing out the big hole in the ceiling to the builders. He seemed to be telling them just how serious the damage was, and they were nodding and frowning. Eventually, the tall man noticed Bianca. He stared down at her in horror, as though he'd never seen such a creature before.

It was most unusual. Bianca was very good at making people love her. The Old Man *always* tickled her under the chin. Even though it was his job to look after the museum cats, he could be quite grumpy and sometimes the cats thought he didn't like them very much. But Bianca always made him smile when she purred – which he certainly never did for any of the others.

"Who's that?" Peter whispered to Boris.

"The Museum Director. He's very serious. And very important."

The Museum Director glared at Bianca and sniffed. Then he sneezed, loudly. Another cloud of dust shimmered down from the ceiling and the people on top of the tower gave the hole worried looks.

The Director muttered something and then picked Bianca up at arms' length – as though she smelled bad! He marched over to the ladder and handed her down to one of the museum staff.

"They're throwing her out!" Boris whispered to Peter, laying his ears flat and edging back under a dust sheet.

Peter squished in next to him. "I don't believe it…"

Bianca didn't believe it either. The museum worker hurried out with her and dumped her in the middle of the Roman Room. The white kitten stood there for a moment, her tail fluffed up like a brush. No one treated her like that! Not ever!

"She's furious," Peter breathed. He could see Tasha watching from behind a huge granite lion. She looked just as shocked as they were.

"We'd better not let her know we saw," Boris muttered. "She'd never forgive us."

They squished right back against the wall and watched as Bianca stalked proudly out of the room, the fury crackling off her fur.

"Now that really is bad luck!" Boris said, shuddering. "We'd better find someone to tell her how beautiful she is. And fast."

"That's interesting," hissed a watching rat, his whiskers peeking round the side of a display case. "Very interesting indeed. That tall one's important. And he doesn't like those little cats, no, he doesn't. And if there's no cats in the gallery…"

"Out we come!" squeaked the smaller rat from the other side of the case.

❧ Chapter Three ❧

Even after the builders had got rid of
Bianca, the other kittens kept sneaking
back to check up on the work in the
Egyptian Gallery that day. It was
fascinating – even more fascinating
because they weren't really supposed to
be there.

They had to stay out of the way of
all the staff and especially the Museum

Director, who was marching about shouting at people. They kept on having to dodge Smoke and Grandpa Ivan and the other cats too – no one seemed to want a bunch of kittens getting in the way. But Boris kept finding new power tools to drool over, and Tasha and Peter wanted to keep an eye on all the treasures up there with the dust and dirt and piles of plaster.

And to keep an eye on the rats.

Boris had been telling the others for ages about the huge rats he'd seen in the tunnels and behind statues, and how he'd nearly almost caught them. But now that the ceiling was down and the walls were full of cracks, there seemed to be scuttling noises and ratty whispers *everywhere*.

The kittens were on edge all day. Peter felt as if he had to keep looking over his shoulder – and he was never quite sure if he was expecting a huge rat or an angry ancient Egyptian…

"You know, I don't think the builders actually like working in the museum," Tasha told the others at breakfast the next morning. Once again they had only been given cat biscuits and Boris was eating them with a pained look.

"What do you mean?" Peter asked indignantly. Even though he was still quite new to being a museum cat, he felt very protective of his home.

"I heard one of them say that the Egyptian Gallery was spooky!" Tasha shook her head sadly.

The other three kittens stared at her.

"There's a haunted papyrus in there, Tasha!" Boris pointed out, licking crumbs off his whiskers. "Of course it's spooky! Look at everything that's gone wrong since it turned up. Plus the gallery's full of enormous stone coffins!"

"That papyrus is not haunted!" Tasha adored living in the museum and finding out about all the exhibits – but even she was starting to feel doubtful about

43

the *Book of the Dead*. She shuffled her paws. "And the coffins and mummies are so beautiful…" she added, looking round at them all. "You really think they're spooky? I mean, I suppose the cat mummies are…"

"Uuuughhhh…" Bianca shuddered. "Don't talk about them. They make my whiskers twitch."

"And those jars!" Boris looked gloomily around the cellar. The museum's collection of ancient canopic jars was lined up along one wall now. "It's putting me off my breakfast, knowing that all those brains are over there."

"Not brains, Boris!" Tasha said, sounding shocked. "Only the stomachs, livers, lungs and intestines went in the jars. The ancient Egyptians drained the brains out of people's noses and threw them away."

"You're not helping!" Boris stopped eating and sat back, gazing at his bowl sadly.

Tasha licked her nose, then stepped away from her bowl too. "Yes. I'm not very hungry now either. But we shouldn't be scared of them, you know. The bodies and – er – bits – they're all thousands of years old."

"Really old, powerful spooks then!" Bianca shivered. "I'm not surprised the builders don't like being here. What if it's not just the curse on that papyrus? I expect the mummies are really fed up with being disturbed too. I bet they're furious!"

All four kittens looked sideways at the canopic jars and the painted mummy case that was now standing in the corner of the cellar. Without realizing what they were doing, they edged a little closer so they could feel the warmth of each other's fur.

"The ancient Egyptians really liked cats!" Tasha said firmly, but she was still pressed close against Peter. "They worshipped them! We're being silly."

Peter nodded. "Even if ghosts did start popping out of all those mummy cases, they'd *love* us."

"I think it's our duty to go and keep an eye on the builders," Boris said firmly. He glanced quickly at the jars again. "And I'd rather be up there than down here…"

The builders were hot and grumpy and fed up. The hole in the ceiling was something to do with leaking water pipes making the plaster go all soggy. Every single one of the pipes had to be carefully checked to make sure they weren't rusting and it looked like a long, fiddly job. Plus, every time the builders turned round, there was someone from the museum panicking about them damaging the priceless treasures.

"This job's getting on my nerves," one of them muttered as they perched on the edge of a packing case to drink a cup of tea.

"Mr High and Mighty the Museum Director made very sure to tell us that there absolutely definitely wasn't anything weird going on, didn't he?" his mate replied, glancing over his shoulder at the heavy glass case with the papyrus inside. It was just too solid to move out of the gallery. "The sooner we get out of here the better."

"Let's keep out of their way," Tasha said, as the four kittens peered out from under one of the dust sheets.

"Hmf." Bianca stuck her nose out and glared. "Horrible people!" She was still upset about being thrown out of the gallery the day before but she'd finally come upstairs with the others because she hadn't wanted to be left alone in the cellars. The carved faces on top of the canopic jars seemed to keep looking at her. All the cats down there were asleep after their night shift guarding against the rats, and their cellar home felt strangely quiet and empty.

One of the builders shuddered and nudged the other. "You see that? Those dust sheets are moving. I don't like this place. Gives me the heebie-jeebies."

"You're not the only one," his mate agreed. "Let's get on with those pipes."

"Gosh…" Boris edged out past Bianca. "Look at that, he's got a blowtorch!"

"Boris, come back!" the others whispered.

But the ginger kitten was entranced. The builders had gone back to cutting out the broken pieces of pipe now, and the blue flame of the blowtorch hissed and roared in the most exciting way. He padded over to look, darting from one shrouded plinth to another. But as he got closer to the builders and their tools, he was too interested to be careful.

"Boris! We're supposed to keep out of their way!" Tasha mewed worriedly.

"Look at him, he's right in the middle

of the gallery," Peter squeaked. "They'll see him any minute!"

It would have been better if the builder with the blowtorch *had* seen Boris. As it was, when he switched off the blowtorch and stepped back to check how the pipe was looking he fell straight over the kitten instead.

Boris shot out of the gallery with a squeal and the builder landed flat on his back in the middle of the floor. "What was that?" he yelled.

The other men were laughing too hard to answer him properly but eventually one of them managed to explain that it was a cat.

The builder went on shouting about it for quite a while.

"I told you they were horrible," Bianca said smugly as the four kittens lurked in the Roman Room, listening to the stomping and yelling from inside the Egyptian Gallery.

"He sat on me! I was nearly squashed flat!" Boris held up one shaking paw and then the other, gazing at them as if he thought they might fall off. "I mean, I know I'm accident-prone but that man had a blowtorch! He could've set the whole museum on fire."

"He'd turned it off before he fell over you." Bianca rolled her eyes. "And actually, it was your fault."

"Was not!"

The white kitten shrugged and Boris glanced round at the others.

"It wasn't!" Boris insisted.

Tasha wrinkled her nose. "You did creep up behind him," she told her brother gently. "I don't see how he was supposed to know that you were there."

"*What* is going on here?" Grandpa Ivan stalked into the Roman Room with his fur all on end. It looked as though he'd been woken up from a nap. "I could hear the shouting three rooms away. Oh, it's *you* again…" he said, glaring at Boris. "What did you do this time?"

"I was only looking at the blowtorch," Boris said in a small voice.

"The *what*?" The fur lifted along Grandpa Ivan's spine and he whisked round to stare at the Egyptian Gallery in horror, obviously expecting flames to billow out any moment.

"It's all right, it was off when that man fell over Boris," Tasha explained helpfully.

"Oh, good gracious," Old Ivan growled. "Enough. I don't want to hear any more! You're confined to the cellars, the lot of you! Downstairs, now, at the double!"

Chapter Four

The kittens spent the rest of the day holed
up in the cellars, trying not to imagine
that the canopic jars were watching them.
Boris sat curled in a ball with his tail
over his ears, while Tasha and Peter were
trying their best to make him feel better.
Even Bianca was nicer to him than she
usually was. He looked so miserable.

Boris hardly even touched his supper.

Afterwards Grandpa Ivan and Smoke sat the kittens down in one of the few clear spaces left in the cellar. The museum cats who weren't on watch were gathered round them in a circle.

"Are we being banished from the museum?" Peter squeaked to Tasha.

"No! At least … I don't think so," she whispered back, but her ears were flattened down. How much trouble were they really in?

"You four…" Grandpa Ivan began, glaring at them.

Boris jumped up. "I'm sorry! It was all my fault!" he gabbled. "Please don't be angry with Tasha and Bianca and Peter. I only wanted to see how a blowtorch worked."

Smoke sighed, and Grandpa Ivan said, "Hmf!" and all the cats sitting around them seemed to shift and stretch. Suddenly the underground room felt warmer.

"You are an absolute nuisance," Smoke told her biggest kitten, but then she licked his ears so it didn't feel as though she was really that cross.

"Those kittens need something to do," one of the other cats suggested. He was a long-legged tabby with thickly marked dark stripes over a brownish coat and bright yellow eyes. "They're getting older. They should be too busy to fool about tripping up builders."

"We don't fool," Tasha said to Peter under her breath.

"Can we guard the Egyptian Gallery? Please?" Boris begged. "The rats have it staked out. We keep on hearing them! I'm sure they're after that papyrus, or maybe the builders' packed lunches…"

The other three kittens nodded eagerly.

The dark-striped tabby cat looked thoughtful. "I have noticed quite a few rats close to the Egyptian Gallery when

I've been on my shift."

The other museum cats began to murmur.

"Mm-hm."

"We could do with some extra lookouts…"

"Those rats are getting cheeky."

"And the kittens *have* been improving their hunting skills," Smoke put in.

Grandpa Ivan looked grim. "Very well then. Tonight, you can have your first shift as museum cats." He eyed the four of them fiercely. "You'd better not let me down!"

Tasha was keeping watch from a packing case next to the statue of Bastet. She was sitting tall, her head held high like the cat goddess. She knew she was only a scruffy tabby kitten, and not an Egyptian goddess – but tonight she was guarding the gallery!

The kittens were under strict orders to watch for rats creeping in through any of the huge holes that the builders had made in the walls, the floor, the ceiling… But so far, no one had seen anything.

The goddess statue seemed to be staring at the glass case with the papyrus and Tasha

stared at it too. The dust
sheet covering the case had
slipped a bit and she could
see the picture writing
– strange little squiggles
and figures. Except … she
could make out some of
the pictures. If she squinted
sideways, wasn't that faded
scribble there a cat? There
was definitely a cat in the
little painting in the corner
too. She needed to have a proper look
later on. Perhaps if there was a curse, they
could find out how to get rid of it?

Tasha leaned out round the plinth
to catch Boris's eye. "Anything?" she
mouthed.

Boris shook his head. He was just as proud of their new job as Tasha was, but he'd been hoping for a bit more excitement. He huffed out a sigh and fixed his eyes back on the hole in the wall he was supposed to be guarding.

It was a very boring hole.

So boring that he kept imagining little ratty whiskers poking through it. There they were again. Every time he looked closer they turned out to be dust, or a trick of the light. Boris narrowed his eyes and glared at the whiskers.

This time, they didn't disappear. In fact, they came a little closer and behind them was a pinkish ratty nose.

"There's a … there's a—" Boris let out a stifled mew. Now that the big moment had finally arrived, he was just too shocked to say anything. "Rat … rat!" Boris whispered. "There's a rat! Oh my!"

The rat smirked at him. No, it full-on *grinned*. Obviously it could see that Boris didn't know what to do.

"Hello, small cat…" it hissed.

"I am *not* small!" Boris hissed back. He was quite a lot bigger than the rat, for a start. Furious, he charged head-on at the hole and the surprised rat shot back inside the wall again as Boris thumped into him.

"Boris! Boris!" The other kittens hurried over.

"Are you all right?" Peter asked worriedly. "You hit the wall!"

"There … was … a … rat!" Boris mumbled. His head was spinning a bit but he blinked hard and peered back at the others. "I chased away a rat. I really did. It had whiskers…"

"A real one?" Tasha gasped. They had been told about rats so often but this was the first time any of them had actually chased one.

"We should tell Ma!" Bianca cried. "I'll go!" She darted away, a little white shape shooting through the dust sheets.

Boris attempted to focus – there seemed to be far too many kittens in front of him. Tasha and Peter leaned against him, lovingly propping him up. "A real rat…" he muttered.

Inside a battered old bit of guttering on the outside wall of the museum, the rat that Boris had biffed sat nursing his whiskers. "They're everywhere," he hissed to the rest of his gang. "Little furry stripey cats. Little nuisances. I thought that tall chap had got rid of them at last, but they're still all over the place and growing bigger every day!" He twitched his whiskers and groaned. "My nose will never be the same again. It could be broken!"

"Stop whining, Luther," another rat muttered. "So we can't get back in through that hole now. Drat it. We should have made an all-out assault last night, like I told you! But you insisted on having a celebration cheese sandwich party behind the café bins instead. What about going through the wall on the other side?"

"They've got those small cats watching

everywhere now, Morris, I tell you! Ow, my nose!"

"They really don't want us getting at that delicious bit of paper," Morris said resentfully.

"What about the pipes?" suggested a small brown rat, and the others turned to stare at her.

"What *about* the pipes, Dusty?"

"Well, that's why there are holes in the walls. Those builders have found cracks in the pipes and that's what made the ceiling fall down. They've turned off all the water now, haven't they?"

"What's that got to with anything?" Luther growled. His sore nose was making him very bad-tempered. Plus he was still embarrassed about being chased off by a kitten.

"If the pipes are so old and rusty and thin that they need builders to mend them, why shouldn't *we* scramble along inside the pipe and nibble through?" the little brown rat suggested, her eyes bright with excitement. "It wouldn't be hard. Not if we all took turns. And if we nibbled a hole in exactly the right place we could come out of the pipe next to the glass case with that special delicious paper."

"Hmmm." The other rats looked thoughtful.

"We'd have to make sure we were in the right pipe," Dusty added. "We mustn't get ourselves turned round and end up in the wrong one, or we'll get soaked."

"Pffft. Yes, of course." Luther sat up and sniffed, and then clapped a paw to his nose. "Easy. Oh, it's almost in our claws, my dears. The dinner to end all dinners!"

❧ Chapter Five ❧

"Those little cats are still there!"
Luther muttered as the gang of rats
peered through their nibbled hole
later that night. They had managed to
chew through the pipe and then the
plasterboard in just the right place and
Dusty was looking very pleased with
herself. "All over the gallery. Look, there's
the white one, curled up in the dust

sheets on top of that packing case. The little cats are usually tucked up downstairs in the cellars by this time."

"That paper must be really special if they're leaving cats here to guard it overnight," Dusty said, leaning out of the rusty pipe.

"How are we going to get at it?" Morris asked, eyeing the chunky glass case below.

Dusty turned back, looking worried. "Hmm… You're right. It is a bit – um – solid, isn't it?"

"Exactly," said Morris, looking smug. He didn't like it when Dusty was cleverer than he was.

"What's actually so special about that bit of paper?" asked Pip, the youngest rat, who wasn't usually brave enough to say anything.

The other rats looked at him witheringly.

"It's very old," said Morris.

"And – er – special…" said Dusty.

Luther heaved a massive sigh. "Are you lot telling me that we can't get in that case, and even if we could, it's just a bit of old paper?"

"Um. Maybe?" Morris shifted his paws nervously, hoping Luther wasn't going to have one of his shouty moments. "I don't know why the cats are making such a fuss about it, to be honest."

"They do like old things…" Dusty sighed. "The whole building's full of old stuff. I don't understand cats, I really don't."

"Or people." All the rats shook their heads sadly. Then Dusty twitched her whiskers.

"There's a noise…"

"Little cats snoring?" Luther smirked. "Some guards they are. That white one's definitely asleep."

"No… A sort of … *wet* noise."

"Wet? Like … watery?" The rats

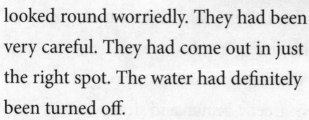

looked round worriedly. They had been very careful. They had come out in just the right spot. The water had definitely been turned off.

Hadn't it?

"Yes!" squealed Dusty, as the watery slurpy noises grew louder. "Run!"

As the night wore on, the kittens were taking it in turns to keep watch so that the others could have a catnap. Tasha stretched out her paws, snuggled deeper into her nest of dust sheets and dreamed...

She was walking down a dry and dusty beaten earth path. It was so hot! The sun blazed down on her tabby fur and the grasses by the side of the path buzzed with sleepy insects.

On the other side of the path the river ran, greeny-brown and sleepy too – it was hardly moving. Out in the middle of the water there was a boat with a square yellowish sail and men heaving at the oars.

In that strange way of dreams, Tasha knew that she was far from home but it seemed that she was in the right place. Somehow, it was important that she was here…

A small girl in a long white dress came walking along the path in the other direction and stopped to stroke her. She crouched down and made a fuss of Tasha, rubbing her ears and tickling her under the chin. It was just the sort of treatment that Bianca usually got and when the little girl went on her way at last, Tasha purred softly to herself. This was a good place.

As Tasha walked on she realized that the river was now higher up the bank than it had been before the little girl stopped. It wasn't far from her paws.

She looked back and saw that the child was running now, chasing after her mother who was calling out to her anxiously.

Tasha eyed the water uncertainly. Was it supposed to do that? It seemed to be rising very fast. Perhaps she should get off the path? But the land all around seemed to be so flat. If the river was flooding, it would spread all across those fields of wheat. Tasha felt her tail fluff out. She scurried along the path, faster and faster,

but it only seemed to be stretching out in front of her.

There was another cat with her now, running too. At first Tasha thought that it was Ma, as the cat was bigger than she was and dark-furred. But then she saw that the stranger's fur was a true midnight-black, darker even than Peter's black coat. Her eyes were a clear bright gold and she wore a golden collar.

A strangely familiar collar.

"Wake up, little one," someone whispered on a purr, and Tasha blinked.

It had been a dream! Only a dream! Her heart was thudding so hard it almost hurt. She felt as though she really had been running along that dusty path. Tasha gasped in a deep breath and tried to shake the threads of sleep away. It was dark in the gallery now and she couldn't see any of the others. They must be hidden away among the dust sheets somewhere. Bianca was supposed to be awake, since she was on first watch. After an hour she was to wake Boris.

Tasha nodded to herself. She would go and talk to Bianca about her odd dream. Probably Bianca would tell her how silly she was being and, for once, Tasha wouldn't mind her sister being rude.

She stretched, ready to get up, and realized that her tail was damp. *The river,* she thought sleepily. *I must have trailed it in the river.* She shivered, still half caught in her dream.

There was no river. She was in the gallery.

But her tail was definitely wet.

Tasha sat up slowly and peered around, trying to focus in the green emergency lighting. The floor of the gallery was moving. Rippling, almost. And it seemed to be a lot closer to her than it had been when she went to sleep.

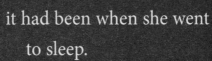

Tasha felt the fur stand up all along her spine. The floor of the gallery was covered in deep, dark water!

🐾 Chapter Six 🐾

"Wake up, all of you!" Tasha mewed.
"Wake up, the gallery's flooded! There's
water everywhere!" Now that she was
fully awake, she could hear the water
gushing from a broken pipe. It sounded
as though it was flowing very fast.

"What?" A dark head popped up in the
shadows and Tasha saw the light flash in
Peter's green eyes. He was curled up on top

of one of the display cabinets, and Tasha watched him lean over and stare down at the water slopping around the floor.

"It's still pouring in," Tasha called. "I can see it now. It's coming out of that pipe just behind the papyrus case. It's getting higher!"

"It can't be." Bianca stood up, yawning and shaking her head. "That's ridiculous. The water was turned off because of the building works. It's absolutely impossible for the gallery to be flooded."

"You jump in it then!" Tasha hissed furiously. "Go on. If there's no water there, why don't you just jump down?" She glared at her sister.

Bianca eyed the water and took a step back. "Well. Maybe there is *some* water down there," she admitted. "I suppose the builders must've finished working on the pipes and turned it back on."

"The floodwater's halfway up the cabinets," Tasha growled. "It will be over our heads soon!" Then she let out a little mew of horror. "The treasures! The ancient Egyptian treasures – they mustn't get wet. The papyrus! It's priceless – it's the only copy!" She shuddered, looking around at the dark water. "The pharaoh *must* have put a curse on it, I believe it now…"

"Typical," Bianca muttered. "Just like you to be more worried about the museum stuff than you are about us!"

"We're museum cats, Bianca!" Tasha gave her a shocked look. "We're supposed to be guarding the gallery. And now it's flooded, *on our watch*." She didn't add, *And you were meant to have stayed awake.* It would be mean.

"Where's Boris?" Bianca said quickly. Clearly she was trying to change the subject but she was right to be worried.

"Boris! Where are you?" Tasha said.

No answer.

"Boris? Are you all right?" Peter called anxiously.

"He's probably still asleep." Bianca sniffed. "BORIS!"

The three kittens heard a muffled groan and then a faint rustling, as if Boris was waking up and having a stretch. "Shh, Bianca, I'm sleeping. It's the middle of the night! What are you waking me up for?"

"Because there's a flood!" Bianca yowled.

"Where is he? Can't he see all the water?" Peter gazed around the gallery, trying to pinpoint Boris from his voice. "Oh, there he is! He's on the end of the same cabinet as me… Boris, no!"

"Keep still!" Tasha yelped. "Don't do that!"

But it was too late. Boris was stretching and yawning and rolling right off the side of the display case.

"Help!" he yowled frantically, flailing his paws and twisting himself away from the water.

Peter dashed across the display case to grab at him. He caught Boris by the scruff of his neck but the ginger kitten was so much bigger than Peter and the glass display case was so slippery...

"I'm falling!" Peter hissed desperately.

Luckily, Tasha and Bianca had already leaped across from the wooden packing case to help. Together, the three of them dragged Boris back on to the top of the display cabinet.

All four kittens sat there shivering and panting and staring at the water.

"Thanks..." Boris coughed. "Thanks, you lot. Why is it always me?"

No one said anything. It always was…

"Let's get out of here," Bianca said, her
[ta]il swishing to and fro. "I can feel my fur
[fr]izzing in the damp."

"I don't know how we can get out,"
[P]eter said. "The builders shut the doors
[to] the Roman Gallery when they left and

the tunnel down to the cellars must be underwater by now."

"Do you think the cellars are flooding too?" Tasha asked, her ears flattening. All those cats, fast asleep… Ma was down there and Grandpa Ivan! "We need to raise the alarm," she mewed.

"But how? Who's going to hear us from up here?" Bianca huddled closer. She looked terrified, as though she was beginning to realize how much danger they were in. "We could put a message in a bottle and float it on the water," Tasha said, peering down at the water sloshing against the display case. It was still rising – just like in her dream.

"Except we don't have a bottle. Or any paper. Or anything to write with!" Bianca snapped.

"Sorry… It's what they do in adventure stories." Tasha swallowed hard. She'd always rather wanted to be in an adventure but she'd thought it would be more fun. And not as wet.

"The guard cats on their rounds might hear us if we meow very loudly," Peter suggested. "Or maybe the Old Man. Except … I wish those doors weren't closed. They're very solid."

Boris looked around. "There *is* a

window up there. Not a proper one – just the long gap that lets in the light from the Dinosaur Gallery. Someone might hear us through that." He nuzzled Tasha's ears and whispered, "I thought the bottle was a good idea." Then he sat up straighter, turning to the others. "So let's try. Ready?"

All four kittens raised their heads and meowed, wailing an alarm call across the dark water and hoping that there was someone out there to hear.

🐾 Chapter Seven 🐾

Boris waited for the echoes of their frightened mewing to die away. "Can you hear anything?"

The kittens sat, their ears pricked. But apart from the steady sound of pouring water, the museum was silent all around them.

"We'll call again…" said Boris. He was trying to sound calm and confident but they could all see that the water was gradually rising up the side of the cabinet. What would they do when it reached the top? "Ready?"

They yowled as loudly as they could but there was still no answer.

"This is no good!" Bianca said, stomping up and down the glass-topped case. "No one's coming and the water's getting higher and higher! We'll have to swim for it and I don't think I can swim!"

"Me neither," Tasha said in a tiny mew.

"Don't panic," Boris said. But he couldn't think of a good reason why they shouldn't. "We have to keep on calling. We can't just … stop."

"What are you small ones doing down there?" came a disapproving voice, and the kittens whirled round.

Behind them, high up in the wall, was a small metal grille, the cover to a ventilation shaft. The museum was full of odd tunnels and tubes, which the cats – and the rats – used as pathways. A white paw unhooked the grille and Grandpa Ivan peered down at the kittens. "What exactly is going on?"

"There's a flood, Grandpa!" Tasha called. "I was dreaming about the River Nile. And then I woke up and my tail was soaked!"

"The pipes are leaking again," Boris put in. "It wasn't us, though! At least, I'm pretty sure it wasn't," he added. "I think I'd know if I'd flooded the whole gallery…"

"Probably that set of damp and panicked-looking rats that shot past me a couple of hours ago." Grandpa Ivan sighed. "I knew I should have chased after them and found out what they'd been up to. But the old legs weren't quite up to it."

"Rats! Of course!" Tasha cried and glanced at the others. "I told you there wasn't a curse!"

"It doesn't matter about the rats, Grandpa. You have to come and rescue us!" wailed Bianca. "There's so much water! I don't l-l-like it!"

"Yes, yes, very well," Grandpa Ivan muttered. "Don't get your whiskers in a knot. I'm coming. Just a moment.

Now…" He edged a little further out of the ventilation shaft, pressing his front paws against the wall. "Hmmm. If I'm careful, I can…" He leaped down on to the nearest wooden packing case. "Oooof. Old paws…"

"Grandpa!" the kittens squeaked and mewed, padding their paws lovingly up and down on the glass case. "You did it!"

"Mmmm…" Grandpa Ivan sighed as he eyed the dark water uncomfortably. "I did, didn't I… But should I have done? There's the question."

"What do you mean?" Tasha asked.

"You're still over *there* and I'm still over *here*, small tabby one." Grandpa Ivan came slowly to the edge of the packing case. "I'm not sure I can get to you. And you certainly can't jump far enough to get to me."

His voice sounded rather faint and shaky, and Tasha suddenly remembered that Grandpa Ivan had come to the museum as a kitten after he'd been rescued from the river. A little girl had found the half-drowned white kitten tied up in a sack. His owners hadn't wanted him and they'd thrown him in the water. It was only luck that had let him wash up on the riverbank.

"Grandpa, don't lean out so far!" she called across the gallery. "Don't look at the water like that. Please don't!"

"What is it?" Boris muttered. "What's wrong with him?"

"Remember the story he told us?"

Tasha whispered. "About the farm and the people thinking he was no use because lots of white cats are deaf? They threw him in the river! I don't think he likes water – look at him. It's making him all … strange… Grandpa Ivan, step back!" she mewed.

But the old white cat seemed to be mesmerized by the slowly shifting water. He was leaning out further and further.

"He's going to fall in!" Peter gasped in horror.

"We can't let him." Boris marched to the other side of the glass case and padded his paws against the smooth surface. There wasn't much grip but he'd have to do the best he could.

"What are you doing?" Bianca shrieked. "You can't jump that far!"

"Someone has to," Boris said grimly. "And my legs are longest. We can't leave him there – he's going to topple in at any moment! Get back. Stay out of my way, I need a run-up."

The other three kittens watched wide-eyed as Boris raced across the cabinet and launched himself out across the water.

"Please make it, please make it, please make it," Tasha murmured.

With a scrabble and a thump, Boris

landed solidly next to Grandpa Ivan, who stepped back on top of the case, shaking his white head.

"What was I doing?" he muttered. "Very odd…"

"It was the water, Grandpa," Boris explained. "I think you were remembering…" He trailed off, not knowing quite what to say.

"Yes. Yes, I think you're right." The old white cat shivered and then straightened himself, glaring across the water at Peter, Tasha and Bianca. "Right. We'd better get back over there then."

"Do you think you can?" Tasha called anxiously. "It's a long way."

"Nonsense!" Grandpa Ivan's whiskers bristled. "Perfectly capable. Life in the old cat yet. Leave us room to land, you lot. Come along, young one. Together. On three?"

Boris nodded, and the white cat and the ginger kitten lined up next to each other. "One, two, three…"

They ran and leaped, paws outstretched, sailing over the gap.

"There!" Grandpa Ivan gasped. "There,

you see? Good work, young one. Very good work." He licked the top of Boris's head and Boris sat down beside him, proudly tall.

"Now what are we going to do?" Bianca demanded, looking up at Grandpa Ivan. "We're still here and so's all that water."

"Yes, yes, indeed it is," Grandpa Ivan said thoughtfully. "So. No obvious way out. The doors through to the Roman Room are shut, which is a good thing I suppose, since they're nice and solid. They're probably keeping most of the water trapped in here."

"But what if it's pouring down into the cellars?" Tasha said worriedly. "The tunnel behind the mummy case will be completely underwater."

"Mmm. Maybe some water will have got through," Grandpa Ivan agreed. "But that tunnel doesn't go straight down, does it? It dips in the middle and goes back up round another set of pipes. Whole place is riddled with old pipes, that's what caused the problem in the first place. Most likely a lot of the water is caught in that dip and hasn't reached the cellars yet." He sighed. "And that's a pity, in a way. If the other cats knew there was a flood, they'd be straight up here to see what was going on."

"So no one's coming to rescue us?" Bianca asked shakily.

Grandpa Ivan sniffed. "Museum cats are perfectly capable of rescuing themselves!"

🐾 Chapter Eight 🐾

"There is that funny long window." Boris walked to the edge of the display cabinet and nodded at the gap that opened into the Dinosaur Gallery. "If only we could get to it…"

"Could we jump across?" Tasha suggested, eyeing the various cabinets and boxes scattered around the edges of the gallery. "Like stepping stones."

Boris peered thoughtfully at the water. "I don't think so. There's a big space in the middle where they cleared everything out because of the collapsed ceiling. I wish they hadn't taken the scaff tower away."

"I'm not swimming," Bianca said. "I can't jump into that water. I'll sink!" Then she looked ashamed of herself and added, "Sorry, Grandpa. I shouldn't have said that. It'll be all right…" But she didn't sound very sure.

Grandpa Ivan nudged her gently. "I'm not keen on jumping in either. There must be some other way."

Tasha frowned, looking around at the flooded gallery. The water sloshing against the side of their cabinet made her think of her dream, the river suddenly rising and washing away the path. The dream had started so nicely with the boat sailing by and the little girl making such a fuss of her.

"A boat!" she squeaked. "We need a boat!"

Boris looked at her helplessly. "There's a clay one in the cabinet underneath us," he admitted. "But I don't see how we can get it out. And it's not big enough for all of us."

"I'm not convinced it's going to float either," Peter said, peering down between his paws. "I don't think it's meant for actual boating."

"I didn't mean that one!" Tasha sighed. "Isn't there anything we can make a boat out of? Or a raft? What about the bits of wood from all these packing cases?"

The cats gazed at the sturdy, solid boxes and wrinkled their noses doubtfully. It didn't look as though it was going to be easy to pull off any pieces.

"This is where it would be really useful for me to know more about power tools," Boris said to Grandpa Ivan.

The old white cat turned round and glared at him with his one eye.

"Well, maybe not," Boris said hastily. "So, any other ideas?"

Tasha stiffened and her ears pricked forwards with excitement. "Yes," she

breathed. "Look! That!"

Grandpa Ivan and the three other kittens gazed out across the water in the direction she was looking.

"What is it?" Boris asked, puzzled. "I can't see anything."

"That's because you can't see it against the dark water," Tasha said excitedly. "Look, there! And it's floating towards us! That sign, can't you see?"

She was right. A flat black board was floating lazily across the gallery, sloshing and slipping in the water.

"No food or drink in the gallery," Boris spelled out slowly, and then he gave a little snort of laughter. "Bit late now."

"You want us to get on *that*?" Bianca asked, horrified.

"There isn't anything else," Tasha told her gently. "The water's rising, you can see it is. If we all get on, we can paddle it across to the gap in the wall and jump through."

"Paddle," Bianca said faintly. "Oh my whiskers!"

"We have to!" Tasha said. "If the water rises much further, the treasures in the cases are going to be damaged. We have to protect them – it's what we *do*."

"Small tabby one's quite right," Grandpa Ivan muttered. "Think of those painted wooden mummy cases. The pharaoh's papyrus! And the sarcophagi! And the mummies themselves!

Thousands of years old! They're not going to be waterlogged on my watch."

He crouched down, ready to reach out and snag the sign with one long paw. "Don't look at me like that," he muttered to the kittens. "I can feel you staring. Perfectly all right. Lot of nonsense, being scared of water. There you are, you see?" he said triumphantly, hauling the board in against their glass case. "Got it!"

"You should get on first, Grandpa," Boris said. "You're the heaviest. You sit in the middle and we'll spread out around the edges to balance it out."

The old white cat wriggled forwards and put his other front paw down on to the sign. It rocked wildly and water sloshed over the top. Bianca gave a little mew of fright.

"You're going to have to get wet, Bianca," Tasha said, losing her patience. "You either climb on the raft and get a bit wet, or you stay here and get *very* wet."

Bianca stared at her sister, her mouth open. Tasha didn't often argue but now her green eyes were emerald-glittery and her whiskers were bristling. The white kitten nodded meekly and stepped to the edge of the cabinet, leaning down to look at the makeshift raft. She flinched a little as Grandpa Ivan settled in the middle of the board and more water came over the edge, but she didn't say anything.

"One at a time," Grandpa Ivan said. "Slowly, slowly. Peter, come on."

The black kitten closed his eyes for a second and then hopped on to the board, pressing up against the old white cat. "It's all right," he told the others breathlessly. "Just a bit wobbly."

"Now you, Bianca." Boris and Tasha nodded to each other. They wanted her on the raft before she came over all panicky again.

But Bianca had clearly decided to be proud. She jumped down before she had to be pushed and stalked around to the other side of the board to balance Peter out. There she sat, looking queenly.

Tasha shivered. Since Bianca hadn't

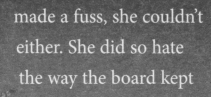

made a fuss, she couldn't either. She did so hate the way the board kept shifting and the water rippled across it. But this had all been her idea. Quickly, before she could think about it too much, she hopped down on to the raft. It shook underneath her and she spread out her paws, thinking sticky thoughts.

"Boris!" Grandpa Ivan commanded. "Jump on. Let's get out of here."

Boris sprang on to the board and it dipped down for a moment before righting itself again. "Oooops, sorry," Boris muttered. "Er. Yes. So here we all are then."

Grandpa Ivan leaned forwards, his ears flattened and purposeful. "Paddle!" he roared.

It was harder than it sounded.

"You're going in circles!" Bianca complained. "Ooooh, don't *splash* me!"

"We're not doing it on purpose," Tasha growled back. "It's difficult! You paddle too, don't just sit there. And we're not going in circles. I'm sure we're closer to that window than we were before."

"A bit," Boris agreed. "Hang on. I've got an idea." He crept to the back of the raft and wriggled down flat, letting his tail trail into the water. "Ugghhh, it's cold," he muttered. "All right. Let's see if this works." And he began to swish his tail to and fro like a long ginger paddle.

"We're moving, we're moving!" Tasha squeaked. "Keep going, Boris!"

"A little cat engine," Grandpa Ivan chuckled to himself. "Good work, ginger one. We're getting there."

With the other three kittens paddling at the sides, and Grandpa Ivan paddling with both front paws over the front, soon the sign was bumping up against the gap in the wall.

"One at a time, one at a time!" the old white cat called. "Careful there, don't let it wobble. Oooof, I'm stiff. Pull me up, kittens!"

And then there they all were, sitting in a line on the edge of the gap and looking down at the delightfully dry Dinosaur Gallery.

Chapter Nine

Luckily, there was a solid fibreglass model of a stegosaurus quite close to the opening that the cats could clamber down. Boris wasn't sure he could face another encounter with a dinosaur skeleton. There were just too many little bits to put back afterwards.

"Now what do we do?" Tasha said, after they'd finished nudging and nuzzling at each other. Bianca was sitting underneath the stegosaurus, trying to lick her fur back into shape and Peter was shaking his ears, which still felt full of water.

"We must rouse the cat guard!" Grandpa Ivan said, stamping one paw.

"Well, yes. But shouldn't we try to fetch the Old Man too?" Tasha pointed out. "We need him to turn off the water."

"Good gracious, yes," muttered Grandpa Ivan. "The damp is getting to me. Yes, at once!"

"Where is he usually about now?" Boris wondered.

Grandpa Ivan's muzzle wrinkled as he thought. "He does his rounds, then he has a sleep on the seat of one of the carriages in the Transport Galleries.

Then he comes here, to the dinosaurs, to eat his sandwiches. Then another sleep on the sofa in the Regency Room."

"He'll be there then, won't he?" Peter said. "It feels late enough. Up to the first floor, everyone!"

The four kittens darted through the Dinosaur Gallery and out past the volcano exhibit to the Grand Hall and the staircase. Grandpa Ivan lumbered after them at the pace of an elderly cat who had already been considerably more adventurous in one night than he had been in years.

"There he is!" Tasha hissed as they skidded to a halt on the finely woven carpet of the Regency Room. It was set up to look as though a group of early nineteenth century ladies were having a tea party, although the tea was disappointingly fake – Boris had checked a long while ago. Three mannequins in long embroidered dresses were posed as if they were chatting over the plaster cakes but there was one elegant velvet sofa that was usually empty.

Now, the Old Man was stretched out on it, snoring gently.

"How do we wake him?" Peter asked, looking up at the large man in dismay. "It was hard enough to wake Boris."

"Oi!"

"And even then he nearly fell in the water."

"Don't remind me," Boris muttered.

"I think Bianca had better do it," Tasha said. "The Old Man likes her. If one of us wakes him up, he'll be grumpy."

The others murmured in agreement and stood back as Bianca stalked across the carpet towards the beautiful sofa. She hesitated for a moment, then jumped up on to the edge of the seat. She stretched out one delicate white paw and patted the Old Man's face, just above his moustache.

Nothing happened so Bianca tried again, patting a little harder.

This time the Old Man grunted and shifted on the sofa, nearly knocking Bianca off. She scrabbled her way back up, squeaking crossly, and smacked his face hard with the flat of her paw.

"Watch it!" Boris muttered. "We want him in a good mood."

The Old Man surged up from the sofa like an angry walrus, making snuffly roaring sounds. He peered down at Grandpa Ivan and the kittens.

"Cats! Again! I might have known. Shoo! Off with you, you horrible lot!"

"I don't know why the museum gets him to look after us, when he doesn't even like cats," Tasha said crossly.

"Bianca! Be nice – do your thing!"

"I'm trying," Bianca hissed. She padded along the sofa and jumped up on to its arm, ducking her head and purring and making little mewing noises.

"Yes, yes," the Old Man muttered, giving her a stroke. "Yes, you're very pretty. Good kitten. Off you go now. I need my sleep."

"Oh, honestly," Bianca said irritably. "Can't he see that it's important? Come on." She reached out, took the sleeve of the Old Man's shirt in her teeth and pulled.

He gave a start of surprise. "Gently now! What is it? Hungry, are you? It's a few hours till breakfast time, little one."

Bianca pulled at his shirt again and

then mewed frantically, running back and forth along the arm of the sofa.

"That's it, he's listening," Grandpa Ivan called. "Keep going, Bianca! Jump down and see if you can get him to follow you."

Bianca sprang down on to the carpet and pulled at the Old Man's trouser hem. Then she darted away a few steps, gazing at him beseechingly.

"Whatever is the matter with you?" he murmured, looking down at her in confusion. "Usually you just want petting…"

Bianca dashed back and pulled at him again, and then she mewed at the others. "You do it too! Pull him!"

Grandpa Ivan looked doubtful for a

moment, as if it was beneath his dignity to go pulling at museum guards' trousers. But then he sighed and came to join in.

The Old Man looked down in amazement as four kittens and one elderly white cat took hold of his trouser legs and tried to drag him towards the door. "All right, all right. I don't know what's going on here… All right! I'm coming…"

Grandpa Ivan and the kittens got into position around him. Boris and Tasha dashed ahead, and Peter and Bianca walked beside each leg, ready to pull at his trousers if he slowed down. Grandpa Ivan trotted behind, nudging the Old Man in the back of the legs every so often to hurry him up.

The Old Man seemed bewildered by
the whole thing. Every time they passed
a door that led to another gallery, he
seemed to be considering making a run
for it.

When they got to the top of the
stairs, he froze, grabbing the banister
and shaking his head. "No, no, no, no,
no. NO! You'll trip me up! I don't know
what's going on here. I really don't!"

The cats looked at each other helplessly.

"Could we push him down the stairs?" Boris suggested.

"Don't even think about it," snapped Grandpa Ivan. "Humans aren't like cats. They don't bounce and they only have one life."

Bianca hissed with frustration. "I got wet! My fur is ruined! Ruined! I'm not doing all that for nothing." She sprang forwards, catching her claws in the Old Man's trouser legs and mountaineering up to stand on his shoulder. There she nuzzled his cheek, purring and mewing until the Old Man reached up to stroke her. He looked as if he didn't really want to but he couldn't help himself.

"Walk down the stairs," Bianca mewed. "All of you! Walk down and keep looking

back at him. Flutter your whiskers. *Try* to
look sweet. Do the best you can, anyway."

"Sweet, is it?" Grandpa Ivan growled.
"That young lady is much too full of
herself, if you ask me. Come on, kittens."
He began to stalk down the stairs,
turning back every few steps to give the
Old Man a fearsome, full-teeth grin.

"Not like that…" Bianca heaved a sigh.
But the Old Man seemed to be so
taken aback by Grandpa Ivan's
one-eyed stare that he
hurried down the
stairs after
him.

"Yes! Come on!" Peter, Boris and Tasha surged down the marble staircase, leading the Old Man past the volcano exhibit to the Dinosaur Gallery. There they leaped on the stegosaurus model again – ignoring the Old Man's cry of horror – and clambered up to the gap in the wall.

"Oh! The water's risen so much," Tasha gasped. "It'll be pouring through the doors into the Roman Room any minute."

"Can he see?" Boris looked back at the Old Man. "Come here, come and look!"

Grandpa Ivan headbutted the Old Man in the back of the legs again and the guard stumbled up on to the stegosaurus's plinth. The cats made a space for him to look through and the Old Man leaned forwards to peer over the edge of the gap.

What he said next made Grandpa Ivan curl his whiskers and glare at the kittens. "It's lucky you haven't been around people long enough to understand that." He bounded up to the ledge beside them and sighed. "But I think he's probably right."

The cats watched as the Old Man stumbled away to turn off the water, muttering into his radio.

"Calling for back-up. Good, good," Grandpa Ivan said approvingly. "We'd better do the same. Emergency call to all the guard cats – we need to check the status of the cellars. We might be flooded out any minute if the water's got through the tunnel. And who knows what the rats are doing. Fleeing a sinking ship, hopefully, but you never know."

"Sinking?" Tasha whispered, and the kittens stared at Grandpa Ivan in horror. Did he think that the museum was doomed?

"No, no, I don't mean it like that. It's what rats do – they run. Whereas cats like us stay and help." The old white cat sighed. "Right. Peter and Tasha – you run through the rest of the galleries. Tell the cats on watch what's happened. Tell them to keep an eye out for any drips or splashes or strange noises in the walls. We don't know exactly what those rats did to the pipes. Boris and Bianca – come with me. We need to wake everyone down in the cellars and warn them about the water. We may have to block up the tunnel until the gallery has been pumped out."

"Pumped out?" Boris asked hopefully. "With a pump? A really big one? Maybe even attached to a lorry?"

"Just get down to the cellars," Grandpa Ivan growled. "Raise the alarm!"

❧ Chapter Ten ❧

Grandpa Ivan was right about the sloping
bit of the passage down to the cellars –
it had caught a lot of the water. In fact,
the dip in the passage had turned into a
kitten-sized swimming pool but none of
the kittens felt very much like trying it out.

When Boris and Bianca had raced
into the cellars and woken the other cats,
they'd found that only a little water had

overflowed and seeped down the rest of the passage. Smoke had already organized the other cats into sopping it up with some rather ugly old curtains that had been mouldering away in a box.

The precious Egyptian treasures in the cellar had escaped any damage, but the gallery was a ruin. Several of the Egyptology department were in tears as they peered through at the wreckage early the next morning. The elderly professor had to have a sit down on the stegosaurus's plinth with Grandpa Ivan in her lap. She had been at the museum for almost as long as he had and she was very fond of him. Grandpa Ivan didn't usually do laps but, as he told the kittens afterwards, sometimes it was necessary.

No one was going to be able to see
quite how bad the damage was until all
the water had been pumped out and they
could actually get inside. The kittens sat
on a wall in the grounds and watched
as an enormous machine arrived. It was
pulled by a tractor, which Boris thought
was even better than a lorry.

"Look at the
size of those
wheels," he
murmured
blissfully
as it rolled
around the
side of the
building in the dawn light. "They've got
to be nearly as tall as the driver."

"Please don't go anywhere near it, Boris," Tasha pleaded. "Just remember that man with the blowtorch."

Boris's lip curled for a moment but then he sat down and wrapped his tail tightly around his paws, as if to stop himself trotting over to the pump. He wasn't really sure what he could do to break an enormous tractor but Tasha was right. He did seem to be a bit unlucky around these things. It was very sad.

Still, right now it was more important to make sure that the Egyptian treasures were rescued from the floodwater. He could investigate pumps later.

"Oh, it's working!" Tasha nudged him. "Look at the pipe!"

The water was pulsing along the rubber pipe that snaked out of the window and through the museum grounds all the way to the river. The four kittens watched it hopefully. The water seemed to be fairly galloping along. Perhaps the flood wasn't such a disaster after all.

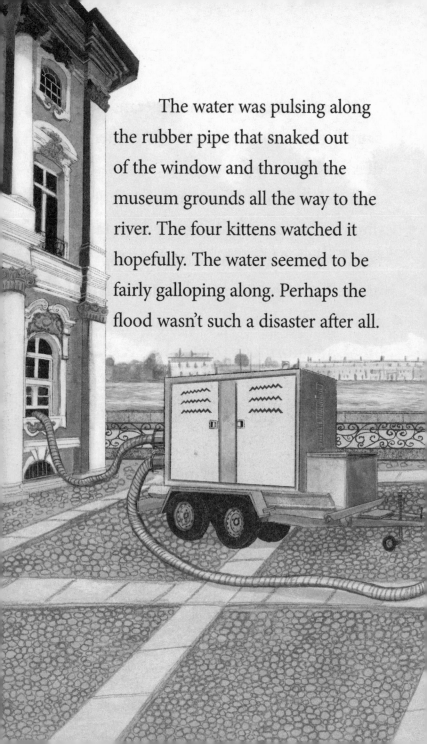

The Old Man was standing watching the pipe too and for once he didn't glare at the kittens when he spotted them. He looked thoughtfully at them instead and clumsily patted Tasha on the head. "Good little cat," he muttered. "Saved the day, you lot did. Fish for breakfast, then?"

But when they sneaked in around
the elderly professor's ankles later that
day, even the kittens could tell that the
gallery was in an awful state. There were
brownish-yellow water stains around
all the white plinths and the smell was
dreadful.

"What about the treasures?" Tasha
asked worriedly, peering at the sodden
dust sheet around the display case
that held the pharaoh's papyrus. It was
just underneath the broken pipe. The
professor was pulling the sheet away, her
face pale with worry.

"Did the water get in?" Peter
demanded, stretching up to see. "Oh, it

can't have done. She's smiling!"

"Such good luck!" Tasha breathed. "I mean, obviously it would be better if there hadn't been a flood at all. But I suppose at least this way they'll check all the pipes. None of the other galleries will ever be damaged like this."

"Grandpa thinks it was the rats who broke the pipe, remember. He said he saw them running away looking guilty," Peter said. "It's a good thing that we're proper museum guard cats now."

Tasha padded over to the tall plinth with the statue of Bastet and looked up at the bronze cat goddess with her golden collar.

"Were you watching over the gallery?" she whispered, trying to peer into the goddess's golden eyes. "Did you save all the treasures? You wouldn't want all your things to be spoilt, would you?" She wrinkled her nose thoughtfully. "I'm sure I saw a painting of a cat on that papyrus. It's true, isn't it? There is no curse after all…"

Tasha was almost sure that she heard the very faintest purr, just for a moment. She wondered if it was Bianca but the white kitten was over by the door having her ears tickled by the professor. None of the other cats were anywhere near.

"Was that … you?" Tasha whispered hopefully to the statue. "You know, I don't think your paws were like that before," she added, swallowing hard. "They were further apart, I'm sure they were. And your tail wasn't so tightly curled. I've looked at you a lot..."

The statue stayed quite still, gazing silently out across the damp gallery. But Tasha was sure her golden eyes glinted – and there was that faint breath of a purr again.

She *remembered* that purr.

Her dream! The black cat with the golden eyes had purred just like that, when she told Tasha to wake up.

"And I woke up and woke the others, and we fetched the Old Man," Tasha said slowly, working it all out in her head. "It wasn't just my wet tail that woke me – it was you! The black cat in my dream

had a golden collar on, just like yours,
and the most beautiful golden eyes.
You *were* watching over the gallery.
You sent us to help… Us kittens." She
turned round, ready to race and tell the
others.

But then she stopped and looked back.
The statue was so still and so grand.
Would they believe her? Perhaps they'd
say it was just a strange dream. She
couldn't bear it if they laughed…

"What are you thinking
about?" Boris asked,
casually licking
Tasha's ear, when
the others came
to find her a few
minutes later.

"Oh … just Egypt…" Tasha told him, with a secret little purr.

Boris nodded. "You know, it's very lucky you woke up in time," he said.

Peter looked around at the water stains and the muddy, silted floor. "Yes, the gallery could have been ruined."

"*We* might not have got out," Bianca added with a shudder.

"But we did. Someone made sure of that!" Tasha rubbed her chin lovingly against her sister's. And high above the four kittens, the cat goddess looked out over her gallery, her golden eyes shining.

Cats and Curses

The *Book of the Dead* does have cats in it!
The sun god Ra could take the form of a cat called
Mau (the sound that the ancient Egyptians thought
cats made, like meow!). Mau fought with the
monstrous snake god Apep, who represents evil.
This story is in a part of the *Book of the Dead* that
explains the different gods and goddesses. It was
supposed to help the spirit of the dead person, in
case they met any gods on their journey through
the Underworld.

There are lots of stories about curses on the
tombs of the pharaohs, but as Tasha says, they're
made up! Some Egyptian tombs did have curses
written up outside but it wasn't very common.
The most famous curse story is about the tomb

of Tutankhamun, one of the richest and most beautiful burial sites in Egypt, which was excavated by Howard Carter and his team in 1922.

Shortly after the tomb was opened, a messenger arrived at Carter's house and saw a cobra eating Carter's pet canary! Cobras were the symbol of the pharaohs and the cobra symbol was often worn on royal crowns. The story of the poor canary was immediately written up in the newspapers and lots of people believed that Tutankhamun had cursed Carter for opening up his tomb.

Several members of Carter's team did die over the next few years but Carter himself died aged 64, 17 years later, and many of the people who were there when the tomb opened lived long lives.

Today, people can visit Tutankhamun's tomb
in the Valley of the Kings, near Luxor, which
is where Thutmose I's tomb can also
be found.

Read on for an extract from Book 1

The Midnight Visitor

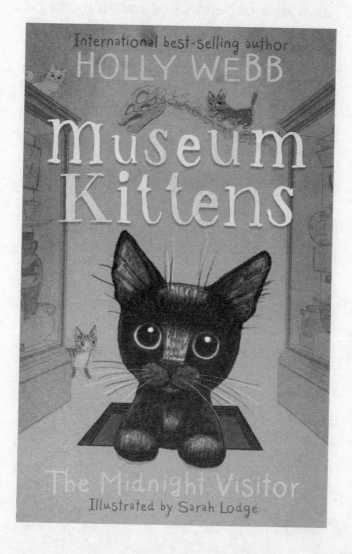

"Mrrrowww." Tasha rolled over and waved her tiny striped paws in the air. The wide stone steps that led up to the museum entrance were warm from the sun and she was so deliciously sleepy. There was a light breeze blowing off the river and she could hear gulls calling over the water.

"You're getting your fur dirty, Tasha," said a disapproving voice, and the tabby kitten opened one green eye to see who was talking to her. "Ma says we mustn't get our fur dirty – we should be clean and neat at all times."

"Oh hush, Bianca." Tasha closed her eye again, but it was no good. Her sister was still there – she could feel her. Bianca was blocking out the spring sunshine and now the afternoon felt dull and chilly.

"Ma says," Bianca insisted. She sat down next to Tasha and started to wash. She didn't need to – her white fur was spotless as always. Even her paw pads were perfectly pink and it looked as though she'd combed her beautiful whiskers.

Tasha rolled over and sprang up, peering over her shoulder at her grey and black tabby stripes. Bianca was right. She was covered in dust and her fur was sticking up all over the place. Half her whiskers seemed to be stuck together too – she wasn't sure how that had happened. She had gone exploring through the museum workshop earlier on. Perhaps she shouldn't have looked so closely at that pot of varnish. She stuck out her tongue to try and reach her sticky whiskers, but it didn't work.

"You are a disgrace to the museum," Bianca said, stopping mid wash with one paw in the air. "Just look at the state of you. Tch."

"I'm not!" Tasha said crossly. "We're supposed to be here to keep the mice and rats away. The rats don't care if my whiskers are tangled. It doesn't matter if I'm clean or not."

"Ma won't agree," Bianca purred, twitching her whiskers at a pair of visitors walking past them up the steps. "See? They thought I was adorable. They just said so. They didn't even notice you."

Tasha considered leaping on her sister's